With Love

LAWRENCE PRESTIDGE

ROLO

ILLUSTRATED BY G. WILLIAM

Matador
9 Priory Business Park,
Wistow Road, Kibworth Beauchamp,
Leicestershire. LE8 0RX
Tel: 0116 279 2299
Email: books@troubador.co.uk
Web: www.troubador.co.uk/matador
Twitter: @matadorbooks

ISBN 978 1785891 892

British Library Cataloguing in Publication Data.
A catalogue record for this book is available from the British Library.

Printed and bound by CPI Group (UK) Ltd, Croydon, CR0 4YY
Typeset in 11pt Garamond by Troubador Publishing Ltd, Leicester, UK

Matador is an imprint of Troubador Publishing Ltd

For my Gramps
(1927-2013)

"No matter what people tell you,
words and ideas can change the world"

Robin Williams

Based on a true story...kinda

1

THE FUNNY THING ABOUT MYTHICAL CREATURES is that for thousands of years now, humans have brought these beasts to life through different stories, songs and works of art; from a fire-breathing dragon to a soaring phoenix, gliding through the clouds.

My favourites are the stories of the Bigfoot. Tales of a giant, hairy creature that appears to be half man and half ape have been told across the globe for thousands of years. Some people claim they've sighted the legend. Different versions of Bigfoot range from a kind, gentle giant that does nothing more than steal fish from the nets of fishermen, to a dangerous man-eating monster that stalks humans from icy mountain peaks. These tales are so ancient and so global it makes one wonder if there must be some kind of truth to them.

What if I was to tell you that such a creature exists? Yes, I know it may seem crazy but it's true all the same. While people tend to refer to the creature as 'Bigfoot' or in some cases as 'Sasquatch', I'll have you know the actual term for the species is a 'Giant Walpertinger'.

This story is about a Giant Walpertinger who lives deep in a great forest. This particular Giant Walpertinger is nine feet tall, and is covered in bright brown fur. Its hands are so big they look like frying pans – large with wide and stubby fingers – and its shoulders are as wide as a barn door.

The Giant Walpertinger has long arms you could swing from and as for the feet; they are absolutely, extraordinarily, unbelievably huge, like giant brown furry trees. I always thought I had big feet (in fact my shoes are size 13), but compared to the Giant Walpertinger's my feet would look tiny.

This Giant Walpertinger was male and had lived in the forest for many years. He spoke some English but still found it difficult. Obviously he never went to school. Can you imagine having a Giant Walpertinger in your class? I bet not. Can you imagine one sitting next to you at a tiny desk or trying to fit on a small school chair? Of course not!

Incredibly, while living alone in the forest, this Giant Walpertinger actually taught himself English by collecting bits of litter people dropped while they were hiking or camping. The Giant Walpertinger was always delighted whenever he found any new bits of litter or bits of paper floating around, especially newspaper articles. He read and studied them as though they were books – he loved to read – as a matter of fact he named himself after a piece of litter he had found and read in the forest. He rather liked the sound of the word on it, which was 'Rolo'.

2

NOT FAR FROM THE GREAT FOREST was a gloomy farm. The barns were run down and looked as if they were covered in a city of spider webs. There were animals on the farm but they weren't well kept, and most of them looked filthy. The sheep for example hadn't been shorn for so long they looked like muddy clouds with legs. The cows were dirty and depressed, the horses were shabby and neglected and the hens looked as though they wished they had never been hatched from their eggs – at least it was clean in there!

On this farm lived a boy called Max.

Max was nine years old and for the last few years he'd lived with his aunt, uncle and cousin – the Whitfield family. He was put up for adoption following the untimely death of his parents when he was just four years old, but the Whitfields became his legal guardians.

His poor parents had been passengers on a small plane when the captain had smuggled his pet crocodile (Clarence) aboard in a sports bag. This wouldn't have been a problem but when Clarence had wriggled free at forty thousand feet the passengers ran towards the flight deck in a panic. This unbalanced the plane, which crashed into the ocean.

There was only one survivor, and ironically that was the crocodile. Max had no other relatives and so had been with the Whitfield family ever since.

Mrs Pam Whitfield was an enormously fat lady with foul yellow teeth caused by a lifetime of never brushing. The few teeth she had left looked like bits of mouldy cheddar cheese. The smell of her breath was absolutely vile. Whenever she was close to you and she spoke you couldn't help but gag or screw your face up in disgust.

Despite all this Mrs Whitfield was still married to Mr Jim Whitfield; a very tall, unusually skinny man. He had a messy and unattractive beard that covered his face with hair; hair grew out of his ears, hair grew out of his nostrils, in fact his hair grew everywhere but on his bald and shining head! Max would always notice bits of food stuck to Mr Whitfield's beard – sometimes the same bit of food would be there for weeks. Poor Max was often haunted by the memory of the time he saw mouldy bits of beans nestling amidst the tangled hairs of Mr Whitfield's greying beard. Had the rats not been so repulsed by the stench of Mr Whitfield's body odour Max was sure they would have nestled into the loathsome beard.

Now Mr and Mrs Whitfield did in fact have a son; fifteen year old Lee Whitfield. Lee was a stocky boy with short hair. Like both of his parents he had no sense of personal hygiene.

Do you ever see people who are constantly picking their noses? Well Lee was one of these people. Max would often watch Lee picking all sorts of disgusting looking sights from his nose. In fact Lee was something of a connoisseur of nose rocks, he liked a crusty bogey which Lee would savour as it grew bigger and bigger before picking on a special occasion. He loved the slippery snot which he could wrap around his finger as if it were caramel, and then there was his personal favourite which he named the 'zombooger'. The zombooger had a hard, gritty, dirty look to it and it lived deep in the back of the nose and oddly it always looked as if it had a story to tell. When Lee had found a zombooger he could often be seen talking to it, asking its secrets; Lee was not the brightest of boys, in fact he was extremely dim.

That foul, farming family, the Whitfields, had been working Max hard ever since he first arrived to live with them. He would chop wood, tend to the animals, pull weeds, paint the barn and do many more horrid jobs. If Max ever complained or worked slowly he received a beating from Mr or Mrs Whitfield. Max had lost count of the number of times his back had met the back end of Mr Whitfield's belt or he been locked in the dreaded chicken coop by Mrs Whitfield. Max was punished for such outrageous things as: asking for water when he worked; requesting a break when he had been working for hours in the scorching hot sun; or not doing his job to the Whitfields' liking. Max hated seeing the animals on the farm looking so gloomy. He often tried to play with them even though he knew he would receive a beating if he was ever caught, it was almost worth it because whenever he played with the animals he didn't feel so alone.

Although the family had adopted Max they saw him more as property than a member of the family. When the family dined on fabulous meals like roast chicken, beef, and sausages with mashed potatoes, Max was only ever given rice to eat: boiled, fried, hot, cold or soggy. That was all he ever ate.

The only thing that always put a smile on Max's face was his book. It was the only thing he owned and it had once belonged to his father. The book was about mythical creatures; Max was fascinated when reading about them and he would dream that one day he could go and explore all the places where they lived. He devoured the stories about such creatures as the Loch Ness Monster, mermaids, dragons, vampires, werewolves and many more – but the one that excited him the most was Bigfoot.

When he read about all the people that had claimed to have seen the beast he could never decide whether Bigfoot was really friendly or *really* dangerous. Late at night he often imagined he had seen such a beast lurking in the forest. He never had the chance to get a proper look but sometimes, out of his bedroom window, he thought he saw a tall dark figure popping its head around some of the trees just for a second. But it's difficult to believe in magical creatures when your life is nothing but back-breaking work and the misery of living with the Whitfields.

Max had often ventured right to the edge of the farm where the shadows of the forest fell and there he would see giant footprints. When he tried to tell Lee about his discovery he got laughed at, but a boy as dim and closed-minded as Lee could hardly be expected to understand something that he couldn't find up his nose.

One day, as spring grew near, Max received his final beating from Mrs Whitfield. It was on his ninth birthday and it happened when Lee had taken his favourite book and started throwing it in the air as his vile parents watched on: laughing! Max lashed out at Lee, which of course led to a beating. It left Max bloodied and bruised.

As he lay in bed that night Max decided he had had enough of being treated like a slave. He had always dreamt of running away but could never bring himself to go through with it. This time Max decided, that night while the family slept, he was going to make a run for it and never come back…

3

MAX GINGERLY CREPT INTO THE KITCHEN. If he was serious about making a run for it, he knew he would need supplies. He raided the kitchen, taking whatever he could get his hands on. He smuggled different fruits, cheeses, biscuits and chocolate bars from the kitchen, filling his pockets as quickly as he could.

As Max ran through the dark fields, he snatched a glance behind him. His heart sank. The farmhouse lights were on and he knew the Whitfields would not be far behind. Running blindly Max was soon slipping, sliding and rolling in the mud. He couldn't stop, but he also knew he couldn't hope to escape on the road. With his heart pounding like a drumbeat he approached the dark forest and, although he was afraid to venture through it, he knew he had to. For Max it was now or never; face the forest or a whipping from the Whitfields.

Max entered the forest with panic running through him. He began to sprint as the branches reached out for him, clutching his clothes and hair, but Max simply did not dare to stop. Surrounded by trees, alone in the pitch black, Max could no longer run. His heart pounded hard in his chest, and he knew he must think quickly. Peering in the darkness he noticed a huge dense bush to his left and decided to hide in there till morning.

After crouching in the bush for what felt like an eternity, Max heard the muttering of the Whitfields as they drew closer and closer to him. As though they sensed his presence they started calling out as they scanned the area around them, Max felt sick at the sound of their voices.

"Yoo hoo Max!" Mrs Whitfield simpered.

"Oh Maxxy my boy!" Mr Whitfield called out.

Lee wandered around in the darkness, bumping into trees and looking rather gormless.

There was no way Max was going to reveal himself to them no matter how hard they tried to butter him up.

"I'll bake you cake, and you can lick the spoon," Mrs Whitfield said in her most motherly tone.

"We'll slave while you climb trees, and you can even stay out to see the moon," added Mr Whitfield.

"I'll do your jobs while you go fishing. You can even ride my bike!" Lee chuckled, knowing very well these were lies.

Max wasn't going to fall for it, but the danger of discovery wasn't over. He peered at them through the bush, watching in fear as they grew more and more frustrated.

"Let's just go home," Lee whined. "I'm cold," he added, as the moon climbed higher in the sky.

"You know we gotta find that boy! He's gotta be around here somewhere. If we don't find him we all gotta start working that farm hard with our own two hands. Who is else is going to plant seeds and pull weeds while we do as we please?" complained Mrs Whitfield.

"Yeah, who else is going to paint the barn and wash the doors?" added Mr Whitfield.

"Shine shoes and chop wood!" Lee said panicking whilst picking his nose.

"In the morning I want to be asleep, not mow the lawn and comb the sheep," Mrs Whitfield added.

"Getting water from the well," said Lee.

"Answer every time we yell!" shouted Mr Whitfield.

The thought of doing the jobs themselves horrified them. They all started furiously scanning their surroundings, hoping to spot Max as desperation began to set in.

Meanwhile Max was panting from fear. His hands were clenched into clammy fists as he tensed up more and more. His legs trembled and to Max time seemed as if it were standing still.

Mr Whitfield squinted his beady weasel eyes at the bush where Max was hiding. He started to approach slowly.

Max's heart pounded, he panted faster and faster and the fear crept into his bones. He wanted to run, to break out of the bush and sprint for his life, but he found himself frozen, unable to move, as Jim Whitfield crawled closer and closer by the second. Mr Whitfield had almost reached the frozen Max when suddenly he seemed to notice something among the trees. The colour drained from his face, leaving it wan in the moonlight, and his sly features were filled with horror.

"AAAAAAAHHHHHHHHH!" Mr Whitfield screamed.

Mrs Whitfield and Lee looked across to where Mr Whitfield was stood, and began to scream themselves. Between you and me, Mrs Whitfield even wet her knickers in fear.

"RUN!" she yelled.

Lee was holding onto his mother like a small monkey clinging onto a tree. They all screamed once more before running away as though their pants were on fire.

Max watched them disappear into the distance. This seemed too good to be true; surely it was a trick.

"What on earth are they running from?" he asked himself aloud as he crawled out of the bush. He turned, and came face to face with a giant, hairy, monstrosity.

"AAAAAAHHHH!" Max screamed as he looked up at the nine foot giant.

To Max's surprise this strange creature responded by screaming back. It looked as scared as he felt. In Max's head he told his feet to flee; he suggested they sprint; he asked them to gallop. He looked down and wondered why he was still stood in the same place. Once again he was frozen solid!

The creature approached, extended his lengthy arms and hoisted Max into the air.

Max screamed, "Please, please don't eat me!" Dangling six feet from the ground in the creature's grip, he swung his arms and legs around desperately trying to escape.

He was sure the next step was to be munched and crunched, but all the creature did was take an empty chocolate wrapper out of Max's pocket. It then stared closely at the writing on the front of the wrapper. Still holding Max aloft it screwed up its furry face and said "Fr… Fr…Fred… Fr…O…Fr-ed-o. You Fredo?" the creature asked.

"What? What did you say?" Max asked nervously.

"You Fredo?" the creature asked again.

"No… I'm Max," Max said, confused.

The creature looked closely at the wrapper again, "Fr… Fredo," he insisted.

Max took the wrapper away from the creature. "No. I am Max," he said slowly.

The creature set Max down and looked rather confused. "Fr…Fr..Friend?' the creature asked.

Max was unsure what to say. He muttered, "Okay…"

The creature's face glowed with happiness and reassurance, and it let out a large groan of delight. Now grasping Max by both arms it swung him high in the air, twirling them both in the moonlight – Max began to scream again.

"Put me down!" Max shouted.

The creature slowly put Max down before saying, "Sowwy."

"Now then," Max said as he dusted himself off and regained his breath. "I suppose I should ask your name?"

The creature stood up proudly to say, "I am Rolo, I am."

"Nice to meet you," Max said, offering his hand out to shake. Rolo looked at it rather oddly before placing his enormous hand against Max's.

"M-a-x," Rolo said slowly.

"That's right," Max said with a smile.

"I is sorry I scare your friends away?" Rolo said as sincerely as he could.

"Friends?" Max said in horror. "They weren't my friends! I was running away from them!"

"And why is you being running away?" Rolo said, puzzled.

"I live with that family on a farm, they are my aunt and uncle and they treat me terribly," Max said as he showed bruises down his arm and back to Rolo.

"What is be doing that to you?" Rolo asked in horror.

"My aunt and uncle mainly," Max answered. "Today I got it for missing the bucket when I was milking the cow."

Rolo roared in anger when Max told him this and the trees and bushes shook with his fury.

"It's okay, it's okay," Max said as Rolo stopped.

"But they is hurting you!" Rolo shouted. "Where is your own family?"

"I don't have a family. I'm an orphan," Max said calmly. "My parents died when I was really small."

A large tear dropped onto Max's head. It was almost as if he was being showered, Max couldn't help but smile at his new friend.

"That be making me so sad," Rolo said in a blubber.

"If you don't mind me asking…" Max said hesitantly, "Are you Bigfoot?"

Rolo's blubbering suddenly turned into howls of laughter. The ground shook as Rolo laughed more and more. "Bigfoot I am not. You peoples are always calling us as 'Bigfoot' but we is Giant Walpertingers," Rolo explained.

"Us? We? Giant Walpertingers?" Max said, bewildered.

"Yes. There be hundreds of us in this world. But we is excellent hiders," Rolo said proudly.

"But why do you hide?" Max asked.

"You peoples be hunting many creatures and putting them in cages or making them dance. We don't wants to be doing that," Rolo explained.

"Where do you live?" asked Max.

"I is in my cave of course," answered Rolo. "I shall show you!" Rolo sounded excited at the idea. "Yous can be even helping me with my painting," he added.

"Painting?"

Rolo let out a loud chuckle "Yes! Painting! Now comes on. You be having much to be learning."

4

THE WHITFIELD FAMILY RETURNED HOME IN quite a state. Mr Whitfield looked as though he had seen a ghost, Lee had a mud-streaked bottom from falling over as he ran away and as for Mrs Whitfield, well, her knickers were soaked, and you know why that was!

"What on Earth was that?" Mr Whitfield cried as he pushed open the door. He was shaking like a leaf.

"It looked like B-b-b-bigfoot!?" Lee said, clearly still in shock.

"You don't think that?" Mrs Whitfield said looking at Lee and her husband with a piercing glare.

"I think he could be right," Mr Whitfield said, more shocked that Lee had finally got something right than the existence of Bigfoot. "How else can we explain what THAT was?"

"Well if that little twerp comes across that beast he's in for it, that's for sure," Lee said, and chuckled. "It'll eat him alive."

"I ain't willing to lose him!" Mrs Whitfield shrieked. "That little brat is far too valuable for us to lose! He couldn't have got far in that forest at night. Tomorrow at dawn we go back and find him." Mrs Whitfield sounded like a general addressing the troops; a general with smelly breath and a shrieking voice but a general nonetheless.

"Are you crazy?" shouted Mr Whitfield. "What if we come across that THING again?"

"We'll be prepared," said Mrs Whitfield sternly. "Lee get the guns! We'll blast that beast. We'll bring back that monster's head!"

Mr Whitfield nodded at his wife as a smirk grew on his face. His wife on the other hand had never looked so serious.

5

MAX FOUND HIMSELF WALKING THROUGH THE forest with his new friend; a nine foot tall Giant Walpertinger named Rolo.

"So what is it you eat? Not people is it?" Max asked anxiously, Rolo looked at him in horror.

"I don't be eating people!" Rolo said sternly. "Now that would be quite horrible of me."

"Animals?" Max then asked cautiously, which prompted another horrified glance.

"Of course no! The animals are my friends," said Rolo. "I be sharing food with them: carrots, nuts, apples, berries… all sorts of scrumptious food."

Max and Rolo walked deeper into the forest and approached a great cave. As they walked into the cave Max couldn't believe his eyes. The walls were completely covered in different chocolate, sweets, crisps and drink wrappers; bits of newspaper cuttings, magazine articles and even the odd instruction leaflet.

"What are all these doing here?" Max asked, bewildered. He couldn't believe what he was seeing.

"Aw," Rolo called out, "I seeings you like my library."

"Library?"

"These be how I learning English," Rolo explained. "Look at this one!" Excitedly he pointed out a 'Rolo' wrapper. "My name! My name! Rolo!" he called out with a chuckle which echoed through the cave.

The two walked on looking at all the different wrappers and articles on the walls. Rolo was very proud of them all. Max even noticed a Kylie Minogue poster in his cave.

"Rolo, you have a picture of Kylie?" Max asked curiously.

"Kylie?" Rolo asked. "What is being a Kylie?"

"Do you know who this woman is?" Max asked, pointing at the poster.

"Oh I am not knowings who that is, no. I find it in a magazine and I thought the picture was very pretty," he explained. "Why? Is you knowing her?"

"Not personally, no. She's a singer," Max told him.

"You mean like music?" Rolo asked.

"Yeah, she sings that song. *I Should be so Lucky.*" Max reluctantly sang a few bars.

Rolo chuckled to himself and gave Max a small clap before trying himself.

"I is so lurky-lurky-lurky-lurky," Rolo slowly sang and did a jig of delight. "I sing it?" Rolo asked.

"Yeah, something like that," Max said with a small clap.

The two journeyed deeper into the cave and Max saw a truly amazing sight. He saw jars upon jars of butterflies all stacked on top of each other. They had small holes in the lids and bits of leaves and flowers in them. There were all kinds of different types of butterflies covered with beautiful colours and patterns. They fluttered around in their jars so peacefully.

"What are all these butterflies doing here?" Max said, rather concerned. "Please tell me you don't eat them?"

Rolo once again looked horrified. "Of course I not eating them. I paint with them," said Rolo.

"You can't paint with butterflies!" Max said sharply.

Rolo chuckled to himself.

"You is not believing me? Then okay. I won't show you," Rolo said with a smirk.

"Oh no, please show me, Rolo, please?"

"I only show you, if you say you believe," said Rolo firmly.

"Okay, Okay. I believe."

Rolo smiled and did another jig of delight. "Okay, grab a jar and be coming along with me."

6

MAX AND ROLO EACH HAD A jar of butterflies in their hands and as they wandered through the forest as the sun began to rise. They stopped by a clear stream with a small waterfall just above it. The waterfall sounded like beautiful calming music. It wasn't until Rolo said, "Here we be," that Max broke away from the song of the stream.

"So what now?" Max asked curiously

"Let me be tellings you something. Where is you thinkings these butterflies go in the winter?"

"I don't know really," Max said in thought. "I suppose I thought the winter weather kills them?"

"Kills them?" Rolo said in shock. "Oh no! You see, when the winter be coming into the forest, the butterflies be coming into my cave for winter. I be putting them in these jars and let them sleep. Then when the spring time be coming, I is opening these jars and as they fly free they is painting the forest in beautiful colours. Let me be showings you."

Rolo pointed out a very plain bush that had obviously been through a tough winter. He placed a jar of butterflies by the bush and slowly opened it. Bright blue butterflies covered in yellow spots flew out and hovered over the bush.

Suddenly beautiful bright pink flowers appeared on the bush, and the withered gloomy branches began to bloom into a bright green. It looked heavenly.

"Wow," Max said in pure amazement.

"Now, you be trying," Rolo said as he pointed out a sad, naked tree. The two slowly approached the poor thing. "Go on. Paint the tree," Rolo insisted.

Max lifted his jar up above his head and slowly opened the lid. Three bright orange butterflies flew out. They circled the naked branches and the tree magically bloomed into a gorgeous thing with bright green leaves and juicy red apples. Rolo started howling with joy, and Max softly laughed at such an amazing sight.

This was the happiest Max had ever felt.

Unfortunately, there was a familiar and revolting trio snooping in the bushes behind them.

7

THE WHITFIELDS LOOKED ON IN AMAZEMENT as they witnessed Max with this mythical creature. Mr Whitfield poked out his long shotgun, aiming at Rolo. With his finger resting on the trigger he knew the second he shot at the beast the family would be able to run the hundred yards or so separating them, grab Max and take him back to the farm.

"Say when," Mr Whitfield whispered to his wife, making ready to fire. He was so nervous he was shaking.

Mrs Whitfield was silent, looking at the creature in deep thought. The wheels in her head had begun turning faster and faster from the second she looked at Rolo. Suddenly her eyes lit up almost as if two large dollar signs were in them. "Wait," she whispered, "don't shoot. I have a better idea."

"Don't shoot?" Mr Whitfield groaned.

"Can you imagine the amount of money we would get if we were able to catch that beast? Think about it? We could cage him up at the farm and people would travel from all over the world to see him. Picture this… 'The Famous Whitfield Family Present BIGFOOT!' We'd be millionaires!" she said excitedly.

Mr Whitfield lowered his gun. "Millionaires you say?" and that foul smirk once again appeared on his face.

"Exactly," said Mrs Whitfield.

"Rolling around in all that money," gloated Mr Whitfield as if the dollar signs had now just appeared in his eyes too. Lee just looked gormlessly at the sight of his parents getting excited by the idea.

"We'll have banks. Full of francs," Mr Whitfield said as he set down the gun and rubbed his hands together in glee. "Dollars, pounds, quids, bucks, cash," he went on.

"In truckloads," Mrs Whitfield emphasised.

"Biggest shares," Mr Whitfield called out.

"Millionaires!" cried Mrs Whitfield.

"But Ma… How are we supposed to catch him?" asked Lee.

"He always has to spoil everything doesn't he?" Mr Whitfield said in sudden realisation.

"Boy, trust your mother. I've got a plan to catch the beast and the brat! Follow me," Mrs Whitfield said.

The Whitfield family all sniggered with delight as they retreated to put their plan into action.

8

MAX AND ROLO CONTINUED EMPTYING JARS of butterflies and watched as they brought wondrous colour to different parts of the forest.

"I can't believe what I'm seeing," Max said in astonishment.

"That is the problem with you humans. You is no longer believing in magic," explained Rolo.

"I suppose sometimes when life seems really dark it can be hard to believe in any sort of magic." Max sighed.

"It makes me homebroken," said Rolo.

"You mean heartbroken?" said Max.

A sudden loud cry echoed through the forest. "Help me, help me!"

"That sounds like Lee!" gasped Max. "He sounds as if he's in trouble. He could be lost in the forest, or maybe he's in danger."

"I is hoping," chuckled Rolo.

"That's not nice!" Max said firmly. "We must help him. Come on."

Max and Rolo rushed through the forest, following Lee's cries for help. They looked around but couldn't find anyone in sight. Then Max glanced up and pointed.

"Look! There he is!" he cried and there was Lee trapped inside a large net swinging from a tree branch.

"Max it's you! Help me get down!" Lee called. "I am in a booby trap." Lee then chuckled at himself for saying the word 'booby'. Lee was a very silly boy indeed.

Max looked up at Rolo. "We've got to get him down. Do you think you could reach him?"

"Peasy easy," Rolo said calmly. "I be knowing these trees all my life."

Max and Rolo approached the tree, not knowing a trap lay in wait for them. Just before the tree was a giant hole in the ground, covered with branches and leaves, and Max and Rolo were heading straight for it.

Rolo's gigantic feet stepped onto the Whitfields cruel trap. As he began to feel himself falling into the waiting pit he quickly pushed Max out of the way so he wouldn't suffer the same fate. As Rolo hit the bottom of the hole a huge thud vibrated all around the forest. It was like a miniature earthquake.

"Rolo!" Max yelled as his hairy friend plummeted into the deep hole. "Don't worry Rolo. I'll figure a way to get you out," Max added as he looked down to see a helpless Rolo trapped at the bottom of the large hole.

"I don't think so!" a voice shrieked behind Max.

He turned around horrified as he saw Mrs and Mr Whitfields ugly faces staring at him. Mr Whitfield quickly grabbed hold of Max's arm and pulled him towards him tightly so he couldn't escape.

"Did you miss us Max? You had us all so worried," sniggered Mrs Whitfield. "Running off in the middle of the night like that; obviously you aren't tired enough to sleep. I suppose we better work you twice as hard," she added.

"Let me go! Get off me!" Max cried which led to Rolo letting out a huge roar that echoed around the forest.

"Don't worry! We'll be back for you!" Mrs Whitfield cackled as she looked down at a helpless Rolo. "Let's go tie the brat up to the wagon. Then we'll bring the cage and introduce our main attraction to its new home!" she added eagerly.

"He's not an IT! He's called Rolo!" cried out Max, "And he's my friend!"

"Shut up you little brat or we'll spank you the second we get home!" Mrs Whitfield yelled as she got up on a step ladder hidden behind a tree to lower Lee from his net. "As for you, boy, while me and your pa take this brat to the wagon and get the rope, you get to keep an eye on that beast!"

Lee looked petrified at the very suggestion and began to weep bitterly. "Watch it!" Lee cried out. "You're gonna leave me all on my own with it? What if it eats me?"

"Oh, quit your whining boy. He is hardly going anywhere is he? We'll be back with the gear soon enough," said Mrs Whitfield.

"It's not gonna be easy tying that beast up. How we gonna contain it?" interrupted Mr Whitfield.

"We can ask it nicely?" Lee suggested before being slapped hard on the head by his mother.

"We'll use your tranquillisers," Mrs Whitfield suggested to her husband. "A few of those darts will knock it out good! Now let's go!" She turned around and glared at her son, giving him a pistol as she did so. "Watch him boy!" she ordered as Mr Whitfield dragged Max out of sight.

9

ROLO CONTINUED TO ROAR OUT FROM the bottom of the Whitfields' trap. Lee occasionally looked down as he guarded Rolo but as the roars got louder and louder he grew more and more anxious and decided to turn his back to the hole and try and focus on something else as he guarded.

Perhaps if I count sheep in my head it'll distract me, Lee thought, so he began "One…two…three…errr four… five… erm…sev…nine…" he muttered, only managing to count to five. Lee really was a very dim boy.

Lee tried other methods to distract himself. These included making a loud buzzing sound, scratching himself, trying to swallow his tongue and of course… picking his nose.

Suddenly a large butterfly landed on the top of his head and then fluttered down to the tip of his nose. Lee looked gormlessly at the butterfly before sneezing, which of course led to the butterfly disappearing. This then made Lee chuckle to himself, but his chuckling stopped as he heard a fluttering sound echo through the forest. The sound grew louder and louder and Lee soon realised that whatever it was, it was getting closer.

Lee squinted his beady eyes before they suddenly opened wider than they ever had before. Lee looked horrified. A swarm of butterflies was heading straight for him. There must have been hundreds of them; all in different colours.

The swarm circled Lee before creating a giant hand formed of many butterflies that threw his pistol out of his hand and then pushed Lee over. The butterfly-hand even wagged its finger at Lee in disapproval.

"AAAAAHHHH! Attack of the butterflies!" Lee screamed at the top of his voice.

Scrambling desperately to his feet he leapt up and ran away as far as he could.

A giggle rang from the swarm of butterflies as they watched Lee running away in terror. You would have laughed too because the top of his muddy bum was showing as he ran off calling for his mum.

Suddenly a loud roar echoed from the hole and the butterflies remembered why they were there; to answer Rolo's call for help.

The butterflies circled the hole, moving faster and faster until they were all spinning in unison. Then all at once they swooped down to Rolo and encircled him.

As if by magic the butterflies gently lifted Rolo from the bottom of the pit and high into the air. It was an amazing feat for butterflies to lift a giant like Rolo, but the butterflies knew they were powerful when they worked as a team. Every single one of the butterflies contributed effort and it counted. Together they were strong.

They placed Rolo gently back on solid ground.

"Thank you my friends," Rolo said to the swarm of colourful butterflies.

The butterflies giggled together. Rolo wished he could have stayed to thank the butterflies again but he knew his new friend needed him more so he turned and quickly followed the track left by Mr Whitfield dragging Max.

10

MAX FOUND HIMSELF TIED UP IN the back of the Whitfields' wagon trying his hardest to break free as Mr Whitfield supplied himself with tranquilliser darts and Mrs Whitfield rolled up a lot of rope to take with them.

"Let me go!" Max screamed.

"Shut up you little brat!" yelled Mr Whitfield.

"Maybe you could use one of those darts on the boy," suggested Mrs Whitfield. "That'll keep him quiet till we get home."

A vile smirk appeared on Mr Whitfield's face. The idea was like one of his cruel twisted dreams.

"Now why didn't I think of that?" he said with a chuckle, pointing his dart gun at Max. "Nighty night, boy," he said.

His finger rested on the trigger as Max closed his eyes hoping the impact of the dart would be painless.

Before he could shoot, a voice cried out from beyond the wagon.

"Help, Help me!" the voice screamed as Lee ran into sight. "Butterflies!" he screamed. "They're after me! ATTACK OF THE BUTTERFLIES!"

"What? Quit fooling," barked Mr Whitfield.

A loud roar then came from beyond.

"Rolo!" Max shouted from inside the wagon. "I'm in here!"

"Go get him, Jim," Mrs Whitfield ordered.

"Me?" cried Mr Whitfield.

"Yeah! Dart that beast!" she cried.

"Rolo watch out! They're gonna shoot you!" Max yelled before Lee put his hand over Max's mouth.

Mr Whitfield took a big gulp and ran at Rolo, who looked down at Mr Whitfield, growling.

Mr Whitfield held the tranquilliser up at Rolo. He tried to take aim but he was shaking so much in fear it was impossible.

Rolo grabbed the tip of the tranquilliser gun and bent it upwards with ease, causing Mr Whitfield to shake even more before he fainted on the spot.

Rolo then made his way to the wagon looking at Mrs Whitfield and Lee with an angry glare. They fell back and Rolo turned his attentions straight to Max. He lifted him out of the wagon and untied him on the ground.

"Thanks Rolo!" Max shouted.

"Now you just wait a minute!" Mrs Whitfield yelled at Rolo. "That boy is my family's property and he's going to be coming back with us you hear me!"

Rolo roared at Mrs Whitfield and Lee, causing them to fall over in fright. Mrs Whitfield even wet her knickers again!

Rolo chuckled to himself and Max started laughing as well at seeing the horrible family getting what they deserved.

But the laughter soon went sour when they focussed their attention on Mrs Whitfield and the shotgun she was pointing directly at Rolo.

Rolo looked scared for the first time but he pushed Max out of the way to get him clear of any danger. There was a split second of fear, and then Mrs Whitfield pulled the trigger.

Max braced himself for the roar of the shotgun, but aside from a click, nothing seemed to happen. She pulled the trigger again, and again to no avail.

"Boy… this gun isn't loaded!" Mrs Whitfield shouted at Lee.

"I know Ma. You said to get the guns; you didn't say nothing about loading them," Lee explained. "I don't know how, anyway."

"You idiot!" Mrs Whitfield screamed and she started whacking her son with the gun.

Rolo chuckled to himself as he looked at Max. "I be so lurky, lurky, lurky, lurky…" He laughed, making Max laugh too.

Mr Whitfield soon woke and scrambled to his feet.

"Let's get out of here!" he screamed at his wife as he hopped up on the wagon with them.

"No! We ain't losing!" Mrs Whitfield screeched. "Lee, you go get the boy."

"I ain't getting him!" cried Lee. "The Bigfoot will get me! Or even worse… the butterflies!"

Rolo approached the wagon as all the Whitfields lay in fear. He looked at them hard, and then made his way round to the front of the vehicle.

"Where are you going?" shouted Mrs Whitfield.

Rolo looked at the Whitfields' two horses that were eating grass unaware of all the commotion going on behind them. Rolo got directly in front of them, causing the horses to look up at him and snort in horror.

Rolo let out a large roar right in front of the horses and they reared and bolted away, faster than they had ever galloped before. The wagon shot off, with them bumping and jolting around as the horses fled in panic.

"Stop, you dang horses!" Mr Whitfield shouted.

"Help!" Mrs Whitfield yelled out.

"THE BUTTERFLIES!" screamed Lee.

The voices of the vile family slowly faded away as they disappeared into the distance.

11

MAX AND ROLO MOVED IN TO the farm. Since Max was legally a member of the Whitfield family, he considered it belonged to just the two of them. Max stayed in the farmhouse and Rolo got a whole barn completely to himself. Of course he put his 'library' on the walls of his new home.

The butterflies played an essential part in restoring the farm. Their painting transformed the gloomy farm into a beautiful colourful place. The fields never looked greener and the animals were never kept so well.

Over time Max and Rolo created a wonderful butterfly farm on their land and all the butterflies came to join them. Max and Rolo had never been so happy. It's not easy to find magic in pairs but the friendship Max and Rolo had would last a lifetime.

As for the Whitfields; well as far as I know those horses are still running scared, somewhere very far away.

KEEP UP WITH THE AUTHOR

FOLLOW LAWRENCE ONLINE:

http://www.lawrenceprestidge.co.uk

Facebook:
https://www.facebook.com/LawrencePrestidge

Twitter: @LPrestidge7